Remembering ECUADOR

ECUADOR		COLOMBIA

San Lorenzo
Atacames · Lorenzo
Ibarra-San Lorenzo Railway
0 ▭ 100 km
0 ▭ 60 miles
Muisne ·
Ibarra ·
Equator
Cojimies ·
Otavalo ·
Santo Domingo · Quito ○
Cuyabeno ·
PACIFIC OCEAN
de los Colorados
Limoncocha ·
Coca ·
Manta · Portoviejo ·
Quevedo ·
Oriente Province
Parque Nacional Yasuní
Parque Nacional Machalilla
· Jipijapa
Avenue of Volcanoes
Parque Nacional Sangay
Guayaquil · Milagro ·
Golfo de Guayaquil
Isla Puná
Cuenca ·
Machala ·
Gualaquiza ·
PERU
Arenillas ·
Loja ·
Los Encuentros ·
Catacocha ·
Zamora ·
Parque Nacional Podocarpus
Macará ·

Kristi Kanoon

PAGE PUBLISHING, INC.
New York, NY

First originally published by Page Publishing, Inc. 2016

ISBN 978-1-68139-816-7 (pbk)
ISBN 978-1-68139-817-4 (digital)

Printed in the United States of America

The characters are fictional. Nevertheless, the experiences of the characters are consistent with the events of that time.

DEDICATION

My gratitude to Pepe, who brought me to Ecuador.

ACKNOWLEDGMENTS

IT'S IMPOSSIBLE TO NAME everyone who had helped, supported, and inspired me during the years I lived in Ecuador, which was the greatest adventure in my life.

However, I must acknowledge with enormous gratitude my family and close friends who always encouraged and guided me in the idea of writing the many anecdotes I heard and experienced in Ecuador.

This little book is also a story about my years there, for my grandchildren and friends who wondered what magical hold Ecuador has on me.

My deepest respect for my friends and Wlady Cornejo and Barbara Cornejo, who shared my adventures in Atacames, especially.

Ebon Davidsson de Vasconez, my *ñaña* (word for "sister" in Quechua) and classmate in Ecuadorian Culture 101!

I thank my friend Dr. Tom Becker, who always provided good suggestions and guidance from his vast knowledge of Ecuadorian culture and professional expertise.

Thank you so much for your saintly patience and guidance, Kelly Crum, my assigned coordinator at Page Publishing.

My warmest gratitude goes to my dear friend Dr. Graciela Helguero Barcells, who, while commuting between Florida and

Spain, took the time to read my chapters and provided valuable recommendations and constant bolstering.

Thanks to my schoolmates and friends from Sweden who motivated me to write about my adventures. My heartfelt thanks go to my teen-age friend Dr. Jean Saleh, for his interest in my project and constant encouragement.

And I thank the cheering on by my grandchildren, Pedro José, Pedro Andres, Pablo José, Mysan, Rasmus, Sebastian, Emilia, and Norea, who followed, with curiosity, my writings.

Last but not least, my children, who always have my undivided gratitude for giving me support and encouragement, Eva, Tanja, Lena, Pedro Miguel, and his wife, Veronica.

My thanks to so many other friends in Ecuador who made such a great impression in my life and I can't name here, but you know who you are.

FOREWORD

I AM NO WORDSMITH, just a woman whose destiny was to live in Ecuador, far away from my native Sweden. I had some knowledge of English from school, but absolutely no Spanish and very little German and French—the latter barely enough to carry a simple conversation. It is not saying that I never spoke or read those languages. I have always been an avid reader and never afraid to talk to people, even in other languages. It never seemed to bother me the mistakes I made, and I never felt embarrassed of my mispronunciation of certain words. By the time I was about ten, I had read every single book in the children's section of the public library in Norrköping, the city where I was born and where I grew up. The librarian took an interest in me and directed me to the grown-up sections, where she kindly, but firmly, showed me the boundaries of permitted literature for a kid. My American English I practiced by reading Steinbeck, Fitzgerald, Faulkner, Mailer, and others of that period. You would think that I would someday become a writer, perhaps, but my big love was painting, and I started out with pastels and oil, learning the techniques from the library books. I drew and painted everywhere. When it was time to think of my future, I wanted definitely to become a fashion designer. I had a special feeling for fashion and what would be in style the coming year, what color would be in. When my teacher in fifth grade announced that there was a national contest in writing and the subject was "What will I be when I grow up?" I turned in a story of my fashion designer dream. I won second place in this national contest. When I showed my award-winning story to my parents, my father (a charcutier) thought it was a bad idea and said that such a profession was not practical, and I should rather direct my efforts to becoming a secretary, which would be much wiser. Besides, the tuition at the art school was very expensive. In the fifties, in Sweden, as in other parts of Europe, reconstruction was in full vigor and good job opportunities. My mood sank to the bottom, where I deposited my dream and donated my award money toward a school trip.

Instead of writing a journal of the trip, I painted wildflowers on a blue ceramic plate. I guess I was an odd ball of sorts, because I always had the feeling I would leave Sweden someday. Once I read a poem about a young boy who at fifteen felt he needed to explore the world and become a sailor. I could relate to him. Since Europe was still in shambles after the war, not many people would travel outside Sweden. Our family spent vacations in the archipelago or on the west coast in Tylösand and the southernmost beaches of Ystad. Trelleborg, Falsterbo mostly. My grandfather, in Sweden, was a fan of Rolf Blomberg, a Swedish explorer/adventurer and a great photographer. He had published several books about his adventures and often gave interviews on the radio. My grandfather had all his books and shared with me the most exciting stories about this exotic country. My grandfather had been a sailor in his youth and would tell me about the enchanted islands (Galapagos). Rolf, whom I later met in person, often traveled and wrote about the Galapagos Islands. When I went to Ecuador, I felt as if I already knew the country and became immediately enamored.

GOING TO QUITO, ECUADOR

I N 1963, WE LIVED in New York. My husband, Pepe, worked about an hour from home, and I was a stay-at-home mom with our two small children. My father-in-law heard about the Cuban missile crisis. Being a military man, he knew that it could lead to complications. Pepe was an only child, and his family had never met me or our children. My in-laws wanted us to go to Ecuador and live there with them. They had a large colonial house and servants who could help me with the children. That last part sounded very attractive to me, also the part about learning a new culture. Maybe I would have time to start painting again. We talked about it, when the day came and I heard on the radio that we should prepare for the worst, making rolls from towels for the floor near the door and around the windows, gather water in all the receptacles like the sink, pots, and pans— we decided to go. We went with the Ecuadorian airline Ecuatoriana de Aviación, as it was called at that time. On December 26, 1963, we made several stops, Miami, Panama, also in Cali, Colombia. In Panama, I asked for a carton of milk for the kids but was surprised to hear that they did not have pasteurized milk. That was a detail, and many more like that one, which had never crossed my mind, but one of the important items taken for granted that would affect every one of us. Once seated in the plane, in the smoking section, near the emergency exit, in the back I heard a rattling noise. It sounded like the door was not properly closed, which, of course, it was. However, it sounded like it was coming apart. This was an old airplane. I lit a cigarette, calmed down, and looked out onto the landscape below that was increasingly becoming more green and tropical. In Cali, Colombia, we were told to leave the plane for an hour; we could go outside. The tropical air engulfed me, but I remember that it wasn't particularly hot as I had anticipated, but nice, clear, and clean. I watched a horse grazing nearby, which filled me with a nice feeling. I hadn't seen grass like that for many years; I had lived in Manhattan, where the only grass was in Central Park and which I rarely visited. As the big-city girl I had become, I had preferred to visit the museums and art galleries! Even with the children in the twin strollers, I used to pack a lunch, and off we'd go to the museum of Natural History, the Metropolitan Museum of Art, or the Museum of Modern Art.

Soon we were on our way to Quito. Now the green canopies below became more lush and tropical. The airport Mariscal Sucre in those days was very different from what it is like now. Today it looks like any international airport in the world. On the furthest side of the airport was a combined receiving and waiting hall that had a low picket fence about a yard high. Pepe's family was standing on the other side, waving and smiling. He lifted the children over the fence and turned them over to his parents, who, with tears of happiness in their eyes, received their grandchildren, while Pepe tended to the task of the passport control and luggage situation. Like most Ecuadorians in those days, we had bought several items in the States that were not available in Ecuador. We had bought a Zenith black-and-white TV, a big nineteen-inch one! It was packed very carefully together with sheets and Cannon towels, lightweight blankets, etc. In another box, we packed the Hamilton Beach mixer and blender, stainless steel pots, more fancy sheets and towels, etc.

Outside the airport was a caravan of taxis waiting for us to take us home. We said hello to everyone, and Pepe tried to explain to me who was who, but it didn't seem to register for me. During the trip to our new home, I was studying the faces of the people in our taxi so that way I hoped to put a name to each face later on. We went through very old historical streets in the colonial part of Quito and finally arrived at the house that was going to be my home for a long time. The neighbors were leaning out the windows or gathered on the sidewalks to take a look at *el comandante*'s son, who, when he left for the States, was barely a young man of eighteen and now had returned a grown man with a foreign wife and children. I am blonde and look very Swedish but was in Ecuadorian fashion, called *la gringa*, which is normally saved for North American women. Some say it is not a very nice way of addressing a person; others soften it up by saying *gringuita*, so I became *la gringuita* of La Plaza Victoria, the square in our neighborhood. In those days, the Indians were quite recognizable because they wore their typical dresses and hats. An Indian woman would call a white woman (or a foreigner) *madamita* or, worse yet, *su merced*, which means "your highness," "your grace," or some such class-related phrase. There are two manners of expressing the word "you" in Spanish—one familiar and the other formal. The use of the formal (*usted*) is when you don't know the person or when somebody is older or in authority. It is a word of respect, not to confuse with the word *tú*, which is informal. However, nowadays, I have heard that both young people and Indians use the latter, not as a means of disrespect, but as a way of the changing times. As far as the Indian women's clothing is concerned, you hardly ever see a difference with any other person's appearance, except in the small towns and villages. Time has integrated the Indian and mestizo population somewhat. Only the Otavalo Indians have preserved their traditional clothes and hairstyles. The men you can distinguish by their long braid, snow-white ankle-long pants, and a blue poncho. The women look like pretty dolls in their long straight wraparound navy blue skirts and white-embroidered blouses with layers of lace on the sleeves; also, they wear their long shiny hair gathered together with a narrow hand-woven ribbon. They are known for pursuing academic degrees, and it is not unusual to hear that they have a PhD after their typical Indian surname.

I am getting ahead of my story, but back to the house the day of our arrival. I spoke to Pepe's cousin Blanca, who had lived in the States, and I mentioned to my husband that I thought that she didn't like me. He asked me why I thought so, and I told him that she only said yes or no or smiled when I said something. He laughed and said, "of course, she doesn't speak English. She understands some, but can't speak English." I felt quite dumb. I found that to be true in many other people as well. However, her father, Pepe's uncle,

Remigio Romero y Cordero, who spoke to me in Spanish and whatever he said, I understood. He was a well-known poet and writer in Latin America, and he had earned many awards. He recited a poem in Spanish about a province in Sweden, "Dalecarlia," that he had written some time back. It was eerie, and I can't explain how I could understand what he said while we stood by the banister, looking down on the patio. I can still see his tobacco-stained yellow fingers when he spoke to me while sucking on a black cigarette. He became a favorite of mine until he died. We had a special connection.

A banquet was served with all kinds of special foods, and the relatives settled down in a couple of rooms on the second floor. They were from the city of Ibarra, near Colombia, and were returning the following day. Our rooms were on the same floor too but on the opposite side. There were vases with fresh flowers and the traditional crucifixes and other religious stamps in our rooms. There was a black statue of the liberal-favorite freedom hero, Eloy Alfaro. Next to the children's room there was a sewing room. I asked why the lightbulb was naked and hanging from the ceiling without a shade; I learned that when there was a tremor or earthquake, it would swing back and forth, thus giving you the graveness of its strength. I learned a lot of things I never had given a thought of before. Like to stand underneath the doorway if there was a strong tremor or, better yet, get into a freestanding closet or underneath a table. In the sewing room, there was a Singer sewing machine that operated by turning a handle, not the treadle kind. There was an ironing board and an old-fashioned heavy iron that we changed for a modern Sunbeam steam iron we had brought with us. There was a chair and a small desk where my father-in-law had an old Remington typewriter. In the further end of the house was a kitchen and a dining room; outside there was what we jokingly called the Ecuadorian washing machine. It was a waist-high cement block with a slanted cement tray, where the water would come out of a pipe with holes in it. It was a primitive shower device, but very clever. You would wash the clothes like on a washboard while the water sprinkled down on the clothes. I used to love to stand there and wash the kids' diapers and then hang them up on a string to dry in the sunshine. I was told to leave that for a washwoman, but I loved to do it while I looked up and saw a small hill in front of me that is called *el Panecillo*, meaning "the little loaf of bread." There was a deep cauldron up there, which had been a sacred Inca prayer place. Now there is a huge angel that sits on top, all lit up at night. The landscape is absolutely stunning, and I drank in the beauty like a thirsty desert-farer.

Little by little I got to know the family and had to promise that we would go to Ibarra and meet the rest of the family. The welcome committee returned to Ibarra after a typical breakfast of fruit, coffee with milk, oven-fresh bread, butter, cheese, and jam. Life in my new home began.

VISITING IBARRA

AFTER A FEW DAYS, my father-in-law announced that he had reserved four comfortable seats in Flota Imbabura, the bus that was going to take us to Ibarra. In those days, the roads were quite bad, very narrow, and with snakelike curves and breathless precipices of vertiginous drops. This was the old road, which took six hours. It was approximately 130 kilometers from Quito to Ibarra. Nowadays you take the new road, which takes less than two hours and is quite good. Times have changed…My father-in-law, as to be nice to me, had asked for the best seat, right behind the driver, which meant that on reaching a curve uphill, I saw nothing but blue skies. If I leaned a bit to the right, I saw enormous steep drops, such as I had never seen before! I felt a stirring in my stomach when we reached higher elevations. I decided not to think of returning to Quito.

Ibarra is called the white city. It was like taking a step back in time. In those times, the streets were cobblestoned, and I even saw a horse and buggy and a few *campesinos* on horsebacks. We had decided to stay at Hotel Turismo so as not to upset the daily routines of the people and so that our children would be more comfortable. That way, the family and friends could come and visit us without having to make an extra effort to receive us. We went for dinner at a cousin's house and had *llapingachos*. That is potato pancakes served with avocado and fresh tomato salsa. For dessert we went to an ice cream parlor called Doña Rosalias, where they serve the best ice cream in the world. They make it by hand in a most unusual way. In a brass pot, they pour fresh pure fruit juice. Underneath the pot they put a bed of straw, coarse salt, and ice. While turning the pot, you scrape down the sides that are now turning to sherbet. (At the end of this chapter you will find a short, interesting, true description of how and where people got ice in the olden days.) When you go to Ibarra, it is a must to have this ice cream. Another delicious specialty is *empanadas de morocho*. They are made of ground-hard white corn (preferably ground on a stone) with pork filling, then fried in hot oil or lard.

Llapingachos: This is potato pancakes served with avocado and fresh tomato salsa. In the States, I use Yukon gold. In Quito, I use the local potato, *papa Chola*, a several-hundred-year-old variety. Boil the potatoes in lightly salted water. When they are fork-tender, pour off the water and mash the potatoes, add salt and pepper to taste. Mix in a quarter of fresh cheese or mozzarella, all crumbled up. Shape to small pancakes and fry in very little oil mixed with annatto, only enough so they won't stick to the frying pan, and fry them until they are golden brown on each side.

Of course, the *aji molido* (hot sauce) is a must. There is always a small bowl of aji on the table, each person serves the desired amount.

Aji Molido **hot sauce**: Put plastic gloves on and slice a red-hot Spanish pepper (cayenne) down the middle, lengthwise. Discard the veins and seeds. Grind the peppers with a pinch of salt until reaching a red pulp. At home, we have a special stone for that purpose, but you can grind it in a small processor. Chop a scallion, green part included, and mix it in the finished pulp. There are as many varieties of this as there are families that take pride in their own recipes to prepare it, but the main ingredients are the same. Some mix in lime and honey or sugar, or you can mix in fresh cheese, ground like the consistency of sour cream, almost, a little chopped parsley and cilantro. Sometimes a chopped hard-boiled egg can be mixed in. Either way, *chochos* (lupine beans) is always a favorite.

Fresh tomato salsa: Discard the seeds, chop ripe, red, peeled tomatoes, chop some cilantro and parsley, and squeeze a lime all over it; add salt and pepper to taste. I guarantee, you'll never go back to the store-bought kind.

Plate the food with shredded iceberg lettuce; place on top the potato pancakes and the salsa and slices of avocado. Some people like to make peanut sauce to serve with the *llapingachos*, with fried egg on top.

The day of our return was coming closer, and with that, I became anxious for the bus trip back. I suggested to Pepe that maybe he could go back to Quito and pick up our clothes, and we could stay in Ibarra! He didn't think that was a good idea.

A few hours later, he came back with a big smile. "Guess what?" I found an airplane that goes to Quito." I couldn't believe my luck. The day of our departure, we went to the grass field where the runway was. I saw it was very short, and I didn't have time to wonder much before an old DC something came roaring down. We were standing in line, and the flight attendant gave us each a little yellow box of chewing gum with orders of "start chewing," because this wasn't exactly a fancy jet plane, and the cabin pressure wasn't always working properly. Indeed, we all sat in long lines, facing each-other, and the seat belts were very wide and kind of clumsy. Surely this was a warplane of some sort. I kept chewing the gum. I told the children to do the same. Twenty minutes later, we landed safely in Quito. I still remember that it took thirty minutes to go home from the airport. What an adventure!

The Ice Merchants of Cayambe: Cayambe is a volcano in the province of Pichincha, very near the province of Imbabura. Elevation, 18.996 feet. In the days of no electricity and, of course, no refrigerators or freezers, the Indians would climb up the volcano to the eternal ice part and cut out a big block. They would fasten it on their back (where they had tied a sack with hay) and with tiny steps sprinted down the volcano and later visited their customers in well-to-do homes where they would chop off the desired amount for dirt cheap pay. There are many other eternally ice-capped volcanoes near cities where the local ice merchants would work. You can find many books and documentaries about the *hieleros* (ice merchants). They were an important part of Ecuadorian history.

ATACAMES

I T WAS CARNIVAL TIME, the year was 1967, and people were making plans to go to the beach. Will and Barbara, our closest friends, talked about Atacames, a new water hole for the *serranos* (people from the highlands). Nobody really knew exactly where it was located, only to make a left when you reach the fork in the road, where taking a right, you'd end up in the city of Esmeraldas. We went in their car, a pea-green Volkswagen bug. Since we were not sure of the road or the conditions of the beach, we left the kids at home, which was a good thing, because it turned out to be quite an adventure. Somebody loaned us a sour-smelling military tent, a relic from the Korean War, and off we went. When we came to the fork in the road, we went to the left, but to be absolutely sure, we asked a native if we were on the right track. He nodded, and pretty soon, we were driving on the beach. It turned out to be the only transitable way at this time during the rainy season.

There was what they call a summer road, but we didn't know where that could be. There was no sign to lead us there either, so we kept going on the beach, hoping to get to Atacames before the tide would come and surprise us. All of a sudden, we felt the car sinking, and we the women were told to fetch some big rocks we saw on the beach. Will was driving while Pepe was pushing the car. Unfortunately, the rocks turned out to be large clumps of clay that would burst as soon as the car steadily tried to ease itself out of there. Soon we saw a man on his horse riding up a hill. We followed him, and lo and behold, there was the summer road. It wasn't bad, not good either for that matter, but sometime later we were in Atacames. The guys pitched the tent and gave us a flashlight. They went to the city of Esmeraldas to wash the car that was totally covered with mud. Barbara and I decided to make a small bar of driftwood and dry leaves. We admired our work of art when we sat and sipped fresh coconut water with some rum, while the sun set in a most spectacular array of colors. It was a good thing we had the flashlight, because suddenly, it was pitch-dark all around us, like when you turn off the light. In the tropics, it gets dark all at once.

The army tent was indeed enormous but had no floor. We spread a large tarp on top of dry branches of palm trees, but you could hear the rustle of iguanas all around. In those days, I was not very brave and preferred not to look closely at these creatures. Finally, the guys returned, which seemed like an eternity, and we went to look for a place to eat. We saw a house on the beach—the only one. A song, which will forever play in my head when I think of Atacames, was filling the air with the unforgettable text: "Las cosechas de mujeres nunca se acaban." It was loosely translated, "The harvest of women will never cease." We presented ourselves and asked where we could eat. It was the house of Fernando Esper and his wife, Lydia, who offered to cook up some dinner for us. I can still remember how wonderful it tasted. Even the traditional rice was exquisite, made with coconut milk instead of plain water. There was fried fish prepared with lime, coconut, and fried bananas.

All of a sudden, a heavy rainfall surprised us like a shower. I took the opportunity to wash my hair, which was very sticky from dust and the humidity, and stuck my head out from the veranda. It felt great, because the pressure was better than the water pressure in Quito in those days! The next few days, we walked on the beaches and swam in the wonderful ocean. Of course, we ate the delicious and exotic local food, mostly based on coconut, lime, and of course, fresh seafood. We drank coconut water, which is the most refreshing beverage you can drink in a hot climate. A suntan lotion of Coca-Cola and coconut oil turned out to be very effective! We explored the many caves where pirates had hidden their stash in the previous centuries. There are many legends of famous pirates such as Drake, Dominguez, and others who, during their resting periods in the Galapagos Islands, would cure themselves of injuries and disease. The most secure place to hide their stash was in the numerous caves on the whole Pacific coast of Ecuador. At sunset we sat on the beach, sipping rum with coconut water, while the huge red sun disappeared over the horizon. It was truly paradise. In those days, Atacames was merely a beach, with two or three food shacks and a few locals who lived on the other side of the river. Today, Atacames is a bustling vacation spot, with more food shacks, gift shops, and guesthouses. Don Bolo, a tall thin man with a straw hat, would take you across the river in his canoe, which he cleverly pushed with a long stake in the bottom of the river. He was always very friendly, showing his two teeth when he thanked you for the fare, twenty cents of a Sucre.

Fernando Esper was announcing that he was selling part of his property. He owned practically the whole beach. He wanted twenty-five sucres for each square meter (about ten square feet; Ecuador's currency rate in those days was eighteen sucres to a dollar), which was not much. An engineer with vision bought a large plot where he later built cabanas, Los Bohios, which is still a popular vacation spot. Too soon, the day came when our dream vacation/adventure trip was about to end and we had to return to Quito. It had rained the whole night, and it kept raining continuously. We arrived at the fork in the road where we met some people in a car who suggested we'd stay overnight in Esmeraldas because the road to Quito was flooded, and they couldn't be sure how far we would be able to advance. The following morning, we had a light breakfast of coffee with milk and a slice of white bread (*supan*) with margarine (*margarina klar*) and a piece of fresh cheese. We left very early for Quito. About an hour later, we saw how the whole mountainside ahead of us came crashing down. Will looked in the rearview mirror and worriedly shouted, "Look in the back!" There another mountainside came sliding down, enclosing us. We couldn't go forward or backward. Now we had to prove what we were made of. There were seventy-two cars and trucks in a long line. The road was a total lake of muddy water and craters of holes in the road. Soon there was cross-boarding between buses, which helped some people from the sierra to reach the city of Esmeraldas and vice versa. It was interesting to see how the locals took advantage of the situation and, for a few Sucres, balanced suitcases and cartons on their head while they gingerly stepped over the deepest holes in the road.

On the right-hand side of the road, there was a slope leading down to what looked like a small lake filled with muddy yellow water. There was some commotion going on, and looking closely, we saw and heard that they were slaughtering a pig, washing the meat in the water hole. Pretty soon a whiff of a delicious aroma reached us of roast pork. We were all very hungry and tried to forget the muddy water. Pretty soon a man appeared with a large cooking pot and announced with an inviting voice, "Chicken soup?" Will asked, "Are you sure it is chicken?" The man said, "Well, it's fowl." Better not ask what kind of bird. We all looked up toward the sky where buzzards were circling, and the bright green and red parrots were waiting patiently in the palm trees. Now we had to see how we could get some water or some fruit at least. The problem with going to the bathroom was a real one. The men had no problem, but the women had nowhere to go for some privacy. Barbara and I waited until dark and quietly eased ourselves out of the view and, with a flashlight, trying to find some kind of privacy, only to be the subject of bursts of laughter when the truck drivers would turn on the headlights. Some shouted, "Watch out for the snakes!" On the brink of emergency, oh, what the heck—we pulled our pants down and let nature take its course!

The four of us curled up in the small space in the Volkswagen and soon fell asleep. I often wondered if it was real sleepiness or we simply passed out from the heat and the lack of food and water. Soon, the queue of cars seemed to be moving! Could it be? Some road equipment from a nearby road construction company of Granda Centeno had arrived to do the cleaning up. Will, who knew somebody in the construction camp with access to a telephone, was kind enough to call home to Quito and let our families know we were okay . News of this huge landslide was all over the media, and we knew they would be worried; it was interesting to see how the men would go and supervise the cleanup crew that had started to open the road. Everybody had an opinion of how to do it. The workers toiled slowly but surely in the heat and seemed to ignore the unkind remarks at times, like "lazy Indians" and so forth.

Then one car went through, and our hopes soared. Everybody jumped into their cars to start up, only to stop again. A second car tried to go through but got stuck and had to be helped out of there. Our mood sank, and Barbara and I decided to make friends with the truck drivers. Surely they must have some fruit there, or maybe even some water? One guy said, "I only have a few guavas, but you can have them." Another one said, "I only have bananas, but they are too ripe by now, and I will have to dump the whole load. Take as many as you want! It's too late to be sold anyway." We returned to the car with a few guavas and some bananas. I had eaten guavas only once before and thought it would not be anything I would eat again. I think they are rather simple and tasteless. This time I opened the huge pod and scoped out the seeds inside the cotton-like cloud. Actually, you eat the "cotton." The seed is large, brown, and shiny. I tried to think of it as a "real" fruit, but it didn't fool my stomach or my senses. This ordeal lasted for three days and two nights. Finally, the road was open, and we all could leave this hellhole. I sent up a quiet prayer of thanks and hoped for a safe trip home. In those days, there were no cell phones or emergency stations along the way. Pretty soon we were in Santo Domingo, which is a small city before you start climbing up the Andes mountains. There is a traditional truck stop there where you can eat something in a cafeteria before you continue upward. We ate what is called *chaulafan*, which is fried rice with chopped meat and veggies.

However, this is not usually known in Chinese restaurants as a real Chinese dish, but in Ecuador, it is common to ask for *chaulafan*. I still remember that the meal tasted so good. Then we filled up the tank with gas and could start our trip home. After Santo Domingo, there were no more gas stations before Quito. One had better know something of mechanics too since there was nowhere to turn in case of motor problem. Most of us in those days became quite proficient in mechanics. Cars were calibrated to the altitude of Quito, which is almost ten thousand feet above sea level. Coming down the mountain, to Alluriquin, the motor started to rattle, and the points had to be recalibrated. The first few times, I had a mechanic do this, but I noticed how he did it and learned to take the cellophane wrapper of a Marlboro pack, fold it, and slide it between the points. With the other hand, I would slowly tighten the points with a screwdriver. If the cellophane wrapper could easily be pulled up without getting stuck, that was the perfect timing! Years later, when I had a car with fan belt, I always kept an old panty hose in the car; in case the belt would break, the panty hose would work perfectly until a new fan belt could be found. The drive up the mountain went well, and we all were ecstatic at seeing the lights of Quito in the horizon.

FANESCA TIMES

IT WAS *FANESCA* TIME. Fanesca is served during Holy Week. At home, it was the tradition that we had at home to serve fanesca on Easter Thursday. This is a thick soup or chowder, all made from scratch and quite laborious. Every household has its own recipe or secret to make it just their fanesca "the best in the world!" Usually, all women start preparing this a day ahead, and everyone pitches in. My mother-in-law, Evangelina, was from Ibarra and made it according to northern style, as she said. The fanesca in the sierra is made a bit different from that in the coastal regions, and of course, each family has their secrets. I, being Swedish, have never heard of this, but I was eager to learn. I'm a true foodie. Evangelina was a trooper because her foreign daughter-in-law was indeed different and had some very strange ideas sometimes. Yet she never complained or picked fights with me; she was a very patient woman!

She was born in a time long ago in Ibarra, in northern Ecuador, when traditions were as serious as their religion. Most people bought or built their houses not on a small lot but on a whole block. This would allow them to keep a cow or two, some chickens, vegetable patches, etc. Everyone tried to be as sustainable as possible. Things were done in a certain way, and modern inventions were not really practiced in those parts or in those times.

Fanesca, according to old recipes, had twelve different legumes, one for each disciple, fresh pumpkin, a squash called *sambo*, green cabbage, a small potato-looking vegetable called *melloco* (*meyoco*), fava beans, white and pink beans, and fresh corn kernels. I'm sure there are many other different kinds of beans, but I never included that many.

Here we were shelling peas and fava beans for dear life. Each bean, pea, and corn kernel should be peeled, Some said to be able to digest the legumes easier. However, I found that to be the other way around. I guess the fiber in the skin helps it along better! Evangelina said it was very important to cook each legume separately. I disagreed and cooked all the beans in one pot. The corn usually took a bit longer. The kernels are twice as large in the Andes and take a longer time to cook. That was something else I had to learn, and that is that everything takes much longer to cook in the high altitude of Quito. My suggestion of cooking all the beans in one pot was not well received, but she didn't say anything yet. When I decided to chop the cabbage in a blender with lots of water, she thought I had lost my mind. With a flushed face, she even said, "You don't know how to make fanesca because you are not Ecuadorian." That was the only time Evangelina said something close to derogatory. I drained the chopped cabbage, it was now perfectly finely chopped cabbage in less than a minute or two. I did the same with the pumpkin and the *sambo* squash. This was my take on this extremely laborious dish. I have made it in other parts of the world, substituting *sambo* for spaghetti squash.

We boiled a cup of regular white rice. Now we had all the ingredients cooked and waiting to be assembled. Two days earlier, we had put the Norwegian salted and dried codfish to soak in cold water, changing the water every six hours. We boiled the fish and made a *sofrito* (sauté), which is the start of most Ecuadorian cooking. It consists of chopped onion—in this case, annatto—a chopped ripe plantain, a pinch of cumin, and a heaping spoonful of peanut butter. The old way would be to roast the shelled peanuts and blow away the skin of the peanuts and grind them to a paste in a big stone! I slowly added the fish broth and the cooked rice and vegetables. When it was all mixed, I added cream and crumbled fresh cheese; if it was too thick, I would add some milk. To serve, we decorated with fried sweet ripe plantain slices, hard-boiled egg slices, and a few little fried dough balls, some lupine beans, and a few sprigs of parsley. I also put a dish with sweet pickled scallions and cayenne peppers on the table. I think that the pickles are a great touch to this dish.

We made it through a kitchen where old and new were woven in a new tradition. Although Evangelina didn't say, I know she was pleasantly surprised. My daughter, Lena, has now taken over the fanesca tradition.

MINDO

MINDO IS A HAMLET, situated in a subtropical area between the sierra and the coast. Segundo Quiñones, a tall brave man, was our bodyguard in the mountains. He lived with Rosa, a beautiful mulatto woman, and their six children. They had been living together for more than ten years and were as happy as any couple who lives the tough existence in the mountains. Segundo would watch over his woman carefully. Not that any man—sober, at least—would ever think of looking twice at Rosa. Segundo had earned quite a reputation as a fearless man in the mountains, where the law of the strongest and bravest would rule.

The Catholic nuns who managed the little village school called all the inhabitants of the area to a meeting early one evening. Rosa wanted to know what it was all about. A nun gave her an information sheet and told her to go home and discuss it with Segundo. Neither one of them knew how to read, the oldest son, Daniel, helped them out. He read slowly, but clearly, that Padre Agustin would come from Quito and sign up people who were interested in getting land for free. Segundo and Rosa looked at each other. How can it be for free? They thought it must be a trick. Even so, they said it couldn't hurt to go and listen to this padre. Segundo wasn't particularly religious and didn't really trust the men of the cloth. The nuns were okay because, at least, they taught the kids how to read and write, especially useful for the boys. After the meager but delicious supper of rice and green bananas, they left their cabin with the youngest baby wrapped in a shawl. The schoolhouse was quickly filling up with people from all over. The men were standing around outside, smoking, discussing the offer from the government in hushed voices, while the women and their offspring gathered inside on benches. Some had already started to weave dreams of their own hacienda and praised the present regime, three generals who had overthrown the civil dictator, Velasco Ibarra. It was really he who had given birth to the agriculture reform, and now the three general's regime executed the plan. They had taken great care to let people believe they were giving away the land so as to gain much-needed popularity. People were weary of dictatorships, whether civil or military.

Padre Agustin appeared, Bible in hand and a briefcase thrown over his shoulder. He sat down in the front row. A man appointed by the government sat down by the teacher's desk. Padre Agustin stood up and wished everyone welcome and introduced the government official as an advisor to the subsecretary of agriculture. At the same time, he made a sign at one of the women to call the men inside. The advisor started his speech by thanking the government and proceeded with the information. He explained that everyone who signed up for the free land had to live there. After three years, the ministry would inspect that at least, thirty hectares (1 hectare = 247 acres) were indeed cultivated by each landowner in order to receive a permanent deed of fifty hectares. There was a murmur in the crowd; fifty hectares was a lot of land, enough to raise cattle and a plantation of bananas too. The dark faces glowed with excitement. The advisor asked the interested people to come up to him and sign with their ID card. If they didn't have the card, they must, at least, remember the number by heart. Padre Agustin asked each person to see him after the meeting was over. Segundo thought that now he would find out the trick. Segundo had learned his ID number by heart and said it loud and clear. Padre Agustin asked him if he was married. Segundo coughed a little, as he always did to gain some time to answer when he felt insecure. He made a movement in Rosa's direction and said, "Yeah, that's her down there." The priest told Segundo that he needed to present the marriage certificate and the birth certificate of each one of his children with all the legal stamps and signatures. He should come back with all the documents in two weeks so he could get his temporary deed to his land.

Segundo and Rosa walked through the forest without saying a word, each deep in their own thoughts about having a real farm of their own. They would not have to be sharecroppers anymore, and the boys could work their own land, maybe even go to school for a few years. Rosa would build a shack and cook for the truck drivers who were starting to come in to the big hacienda owned by a powerful man. Most people in the area worked for him as sharecroppers or peons. Rumors had it that he owned five thousand hectares. Together with his son-in-law, an engineer who worked for the local government in Quito, a big lumber company was formed. He had big plans of felling the trees and processing them in the area before transporting the lumber to Quito. My husband and I were the partners responsible for the transportation. We had bought an eighteen-wheeler with a platform.

Rosa kept dreaming of her restaurant, thinking her two oldest girls could help her in the kitchen. Maybe they could even get married, someday, to a gringo. Lately, there had been many gringos in the area collecting plants and butterflies. Rosa came back to reality when the baby let out a holler. Rosa examined her, and her little face was all red from crying, and she looked quite flushed. If she didn't stop crying after a while, she would take her to the nurse/midwife who lived near the soccer field. She hoped the baby would stop crying because it was getting dark soon, and it would take her an hour to get there. The baby kept crying persistently, and at once, upon getting back to the cabin, Rosa put down the baby on the steps and opened her cloth diaper. The poor baby was all red from a bite of some sort. While opening the slightly damp diaper, an enormous ant fell out on the wooden step. Rosa shook the diaper and put it on again. She was thinking how different it would be to have a real nice farmhouse made with cinder blocks and good wood floors, waxed and polished to a shine, and not these bamboo structures with spaces in between, which made it easy for all kinds of creatures to come into the cabin.

A few days later, a new truck arrived in the area. It was our eighteen-wheeler, and the driver was unknown to the people. Juan Gomez, who also had a truck, did not like the competition and threw out a big log in front of our truck. Our driver had just enough time to stop and skid to the right side of the muddy road. He jumped down angrily from the truck and confronted the man, demanding to know why he had thrown out the log on the road. A heated argument followed, but nobody saw Pepe in the truck, who quietly opened the door on the passenger side and slid soundlessly down to the road and fired his powerful Winchester in the air. The driver and Juan Gomez both stopped in their tracks. The incident was over!

Segundo had seen this and stepped over to the brave man with his rifle. They both introduced themselves and shook hands. Segundo said, "You must be hungry and thirsty, don Pepe. You come home to my house and tell me about yourself." Pepe told him he was a partner in the new lumber business with the big hacendado (landowner) and his son-in-law in Quito. He told Segundo that he had just arrived from the United States with his foreign wife and children. Segundo offered to protect Pepe, because newcomers were looked upon with suspicion in this area, and Juan Gomez had already declared war, defending "his territory." This was the beginning of a long and loyal friendship.

When Pepe came back to Mindo the next time, Segundo told Pepe about the priest and the free land he had signed up for. "There is only one problem," said Segundo. "I have all the necessary certificates, except the marriage certificate, since I am not married to Rosa. How can we get married?" Pepe said, "You can get married in the *registro civil* [city hall] only, if you don't want to get married in church too." Pepe offered to find out exactly what to do. When Pepe came back home in Quito, he told me about this, and I started to mentally plan the wedding. Pepe explained that Segundo and Rosa were plain people and not interested in an elaborate wedding. I had already planned even the dress for Rosa—one of my own dresses I had only worn twice before the children were born, and after, it didn't fit me. The dress was made of white Thai silk with blue polka dots. It had cost a fortune, and I was only glad that Rosa could wear it. I told my mother-in-law about the wedding. In those days, there was a marked separation of social classes. She explained that they simply did not mix with mountain people or people of color. I realized that either side would be just as embarrassed and uncomfortable. Still, I prepared a table with finger food and drinks.

The day arrived, and Segundo and Rosa came with their children all dressed up in Sunday clothes. They brought several orchid plants for me and one very special red orchid that Segundo found in Pachijal, the vacation place of the Inca emperor Atahualpa, according to legends. Pepe went with them to the city hall, where they were married.

With the required married certificate and having enjoyed the little wedding banquet, they returned to Mindo, with their new status of being legally married, seeing their farm more and more a reality. We had helped Segundo to make copies of all the documents and put them in a nice red folder.

After two weeks, Segundo went to turn in the required certificates. Rosa's mood sank when she saw Segundo coming up the path to the cabin with the red folder in his hand. "What?" she cried. "they need more papers?" Segundo opened the folder and waved a piece of paper in front of her. "Here is our farm," he grinned. "Now we have to find a safe place to put this in. They told me that we should bring this paper, called a deed, to the Banco de Fomento (state-owned agricultural bank) where we can get a loan to buy cattle and seeds." Rosa made a sign of the cross on her chest and thanked God for this fortune that had been given to them. Neither one of them felt like sleeping. They lighted a small oil lamp, and Segundo poured two small jelly glasses of *aguardiente* (sugarcane alcohol); they both had "party feelings," as Rosa called their new happiness. As Segundo started to pour another drink, Rosa made a sign with her finger that she didn't want any and that he shouldn't have that either. Segundo thought, "So that's what happens when you get married. A woman can never deny a man to have a drink or tell him what to do." He told Rosa what he thought about that, and she replied that now she had rights too and didn't want to have to deal with a drunk.

They had their first squabble as married folks, but not the last. Rosa went to bed and couldn't sleep; her thoughts occupied with plans; she didn't even hear when Segundo went to bed beside her.

She must have drifted off to sleep in the early-morning hours when she heard a knock on the door. It was don Pepe. "Segundo, come quick, we found a man, badly hurt, and I think I need to take him to Quito." Segundo pulled on his pants as fast as he could, grabbed his machete, and he was out the door. The man, in his late thirties, had a bad machete cut on his underarm. Pepe took off his undershirt and made a rudimentary tourniquet; hopefully, it would help until they arrived in Quito. Pepe asked Segundo to help him put the man on the platform, making a bed of sorts and arranging on all sides sacks filled with charcoal so he wouldn't fall off the platform. We had some customers who would buy charcoal in Quito, which wasn't much of a profit, but sometimes enough to pay for the gas. Pepe gave some orders to Segundo and let the people know that he would be back as soon as he had found a hospital for the man.

Tomas Quispe, a gardener from Cumbaya, a suburb in Quito, had moved to Mindo to take advantage of the free land. He didn't know how to carry a machete, and in a moment of carelessness, he supported the machete against a rock and his sweaty hand slid down and caused the sharp blade to cut his underarm. The road from Mindo to Quito had many turns and very deep precipices. You really needed to know how to drive a big truck. it was only sixty kilometers, but this scary trip was not made in less than six hours; in bad weather, with torrential rain, it would take up to eight hours. Pepe understood that he was racing against time and tried to go as fast as he could, making sure that Tomas was secure on the platform. Finally, arriving to Quito and a Red Cross clinic, Pepe was faced with the possibility of going to be arrested. When the orderlies gently put Tomas on a gurney, he fainted. Meanwhile, the clinic's personnel had called a police, who interrogated Pepe, accusing him of likely having fought and cut Tomas with the machete. It could have been a terrible turnout if Tomas hadn't reacted and could give a testimony that indeed Pepe had saved his life.

ROSITA

ROSITA LOVED EVERYTHING FOREIGN and thought there was nothing in Ecuador that could compare to it. She was born in the Chota Valley in the northern part of Ecuador, but she grew up in Mindo with her mother, Rosa, and her father, Segundo. Her skin was golden light brown and her features fine and delicate, thanks to her white grandfather, said her mother.

When, as a young girl of sixteen, she had come to the capital, she was thrilled beyond words to get a job as an assistant cook in the home of a high-ranking military officer in the American embassy. She was never able to pronounce his last name, so she called him *mi general*, although he was a colonel. He and his family had lived in many different countries. His second wife was a much younger woman with shiny platinum-blond long hair and dresses that Rosita longingly eyed; she was very much impressed by her clothes, her shoes, and jewelry. She had asked if she could have old magazines, which she drooled over at night when she was back in her little room that she shared with a cousin, Gloria, who was the official chef.

Ms. Carole, as she called her, was very picky with new recipes and wanted every meal to be absolutely right, especially when they had guests, which was at least once a week.

Rosita soon learned about French and Italian cooking. And she watched carefully when the chef turned out succulent dishes with flavorings unknown to her.

Near Christmas, she was told that the colonel's son from a previous marriage was coming to visit. The house was decorated like in the magazines, and foods were prepared, and cookies were baked and stored in tins. Gloria went with Ms. Carole to the commissary of the embassy and brought back jars of berries and spices from the United States. It was a busy time with many formal dinners.

Rosita was busy and not even aware of the handsome young man who entered the kitchen.

"Hola," he said, "my name is James or Jaime in Spanish, but everyone calls me Jim. What's your name?"

At that moment, Ms. Carole entered the kitchen and asked Jim to help her with something. She looked flustered, and he hurriedly left with her.

Rosita did not see Jim for several days, although she thought she saw him a couple of times in the garden when she left in the evening.

One evening after work, there he was, indeed waiting for her in the garden.

"Hola," he said again. He spoke quite good Spanish with a foreign accent. "I wanted to talk to you, but you are always so busy."

He came closer to her, and she could smell the sweet citrus and spicy fragrance of aftershave lotion.

"I have never seen a girl quite so beautiful as you," he said and drew her toward him.

She let him and felt a warm feeling, not protesting when he suddenly kissed her.

She had never been kissed before, and she liked it. Jim wanted to see her the following evening again when she was finished with her work. He said he had a surprise for her.

The next day, she could hardly concentrate on her job and only thought about seeing him again. Carole looked at her as though she wanted to say something but changed her mind. Rosita brushed her hair and washed her face before she hurried out to the garden, where Jim was waiting for her. He put his arm around her shoulder and drew her close to him. She eagerly turned up her face, hoping he would kiss her again. He walked with her toward the heated pool, where there were several beach chairs, and pulled her down in one of them. She never felt the pain when he pushed himself in her. It was over very quickly, and later she doubted that something even had happened. Next month, she was late and really worried that she could be pregnant, but it was only that time, so it was probably nothing. Maybe it had to do with the fact that she wasn't a virgin anymore.

When the second month came around and she often had nausea and vomited, her cousin Gloria looked at her with suspicion. She asked Rosita if she had a boyfriend, but Rosita only shook her head and would not talk about it.

In the third month, Carole looked at Rosita with questioning eyes. When she talked to Gloria about it, she too could not answer if Rosita had a boyfriend or not. Soon there was no question about it. Rosita was indeed pregnant. She didn't know how to get in touch with Jim, who had long ago returned to his school. Gloria sent word to Rosa and Segundo that they should come to Quito as soon as possible.

Gloria had not mentioned anything about Rosita, only that she needed to talk to them.

They arrived one sunny day. Rosa saw immediately that Rosita was pregnant, and when she told Segundo, he became wild with anger.

"Rosita," he yelled, "who is the father? Is it el patron, the colonel?"

"No," Rosita said, but Segundo was blind with anger and rushed into the house to confront him.

The colonel was just ready to have breakfast and was seated in the dining room when Segundo raced in like a madman.

"Get up! You have made my Rosita pregnant, and now you have to answer to me," Segundo shouted and closed in on the colonel with a threatening action.

He pulled up the colonel from his chair and shook him, so the coffee spilled, and a button from his shirt fell down on the floor. The colonel was not prepared for this altercation and lost his balance. He fell soundlessly but with a thud when he hit the floor. Segundo screamed at him to get up, but the colonel did not answer. He was lying on the floor face down where he had fallen and didn't move. Carole, who had heard the shouting and noises, came rushing into the dining room and let out a loud scream when she saw her husband on the floor. Rosa tugged at Segundo's shirt and motioned for him to leave the house. A guard came rushing in, and Carole shouted at him to stop Segundo. Rosita and Gloria were huddled together in shock, unable to move. Carole shouted to them to call an ambulance. The colonel still didn't move, and when the ambulance finally arrived, he had turned pale in the face.

Being an American military diplomat, it was encouraged to request police escort in an emergency situation. Several police cars pulled up at the diplomat's residence and a marine guard, who held Segundo in a tight grip, turned him over to the local officer and hastily explained what happened. He called his supervisor, who told the guard to stay put and wait for him to arrive shortly so he could give his version of the incident.

The situation escalated, and Rosita and her mother left the room. Carole called out to Gloria that she needed to make sure they wouldn't disappear. Gloria had not seen the incident, but she did hear the elevated angry voices. The gunny sergeant arrived within a few minutes together with a local employee, his assistant.

Segundo had to give his version of what had happened. He was still angry and flustered. His voice was agitated and came in short spurts when he answered the assistant who was asking the questions the gunny had ordered in English. The interrogation was over, and everything was documented both on paper and on tape from the small recorder the gunny had placed on the table.

With jerking pushes and shoves, the guards and the local police drove off with Segundo. Rosa went to the back room with Rosita and Gloria.

She would have to look for a lawyer who could get Segundo out of jail as soon as possible. The farm had to be tended. She had no idea who she could call, so she called Don Pepe, who immediately got on the phone and made some calls. Segundo had been Pepe's bodyguard in the mountains when he had the lumber business there. They had been good friends ever since. There were quite a few lawyers in Pepe's family, even a superior court judge. He was hoping to get free advice so he could get Segundo out of jail immediately. Besides, he knew that money was short. Pepe's uncle Oswaldo said he would wait for Pepe in his office within the hour.

Oswaldo made some calls and told Pepe that the situation had turned very difficult because the colonel was in the hospital and had still not responded to treatment. He didn't see that a quick release would be possible for Segundo if the colonel didn't gain consciousness soon. Oswaldo made a few more phone calls and shook his head as he hung up.

The colonel had had a stroke, and the doctors could not disclose his present condition, and his wife had insisted that he be airlifted to the nearest American hospital, which was in Panama.

Again, Oswaldo shook his head and said, "It doesn't look good, but we'll make the customary paperwork and present it this afternoon anyway."

Pepe called Rosita and asked how everything was at the house. She said Ms. Carole hadn't come back from the hospital, where she waited for her husband to be transported to Panama, and nobody really knew what to do. Pepe told Rosita to call Rosa. She came to the phone and, with a worried voice, asked Pepe what was going on. He told her that things didn't look good, but he had found a lawyer who was helping. She should buy some food for Segundo, and he gave her the address to the city jail where he was held.

The judicial system was grinding slowly, and Segundo had left word with Rosa that she should call Don Pepe and ask him to look for someone to fill in for him at the farm. He had ordered twenty cows, which should be arriving any day, but before, they needed to put up a fence.

"Better yet," he said, "please tell Don Pepe to come and see me in jail."

Pepe, who always looks out for his friends, went straight for the jail. To be sure he would be able to talk to Segundo, he brought Oswaldo along. With a bit of haggling and the passing over of a few bills to the sergeant, Pepe was able to talk to Segundo.

Pepe had never lived on a farm and had no idea how it works but promised Segundo that with Rosa's help, he would try to help out. He thought that to put up a fence couldn't be that much of a problem. Besides, the money he had saved in New York was safely in the bank, waiting for him to decide in what to invest. He had all the time in the world and actually looked forward to work helping his friend, who many times had helped him in the mountains. Pepe saw it as a payback time and cheerfully committed to his promise.

The colonel had never regained consciousness and died shortly after arriving in Panama.

This put Segundo in a dangerous position, and Oswaldo told Pepe to prepare Rosa that Segundo might not be free for a long time.

As a special favor to Oswaldo, who again opened his billfold for the guards, Pepe was able to meet with Segundo to discuss the farm.

With Rosa's help and Juan's help (a cousin), Pepe had managed to put up a pretty decent fence for the twenty cows.

The day of the sentencing finally arrived. Segundo was sentenced to eight years in prison. They decided it was involuntary manslaughter instead of murder, which carried a sixteen-year sentence.

Segundo offered to go into partnership with Pepe in his farm project. Pepe was thankful for the offer, but he explained to Segundo that he was a city guy and really didn't like the country enough to live there. Pepe promised to find a solution to the problem and not to worry about it. Oswaldo would be coming to see him and prepare him for the appeal process that would start soon. He needed to know how he was going to pay him. Did he have any money? Segundo said he had no cash and would have to take a loan with the farm for collateral. Pepe promised to consult with Oswaldo about it and get back to him about that.

John Swanson was a Vietnam War veteran. After the war, he had taken advantage of the GI bill and went back to school. He was now a biologist and had gotten a grant to study certain plants in the Mindo region. He grew up on his parents' wheat farm in Nebraska but had stayed in California when he came back from the war. There he felt free and had acquired certain habits that he knew his parents' strict Lutheran values would not accept. He was a grown man now and felt he was his own master and would be much better off to live alone. He also knew that his father had expected him to take over the farm someday, which John really didn't care for. It wasn't really because of the farm, per se. He really liked the peacefulness of the country, but it was more his father's stubbornness and dictatorial manners that kept him away from the idea of going back home and which made him stay in San Francisco. He rented a room and got a job playing the guitar in a club. It was a hole-in-the-wall sort of place with a hippie and student clientele mostly, but the pay was not bad, and he was offered a free meal per day. The owner, a large black woman from Georgia, cooked genuine soul food, which he greatly appreciated.

She told him that the free meal was because she wanted to pay him back in some way for his service to her country. It worked out well for John too, and soon he started to inquire about his school and the GI bill benefits. He kept his job playing guitar, and pretty soon he was finished with his bachelor's and master's degrees, and when applying for a grant for a research project, he was offered the grant, which was accepted and took him to Ecuador and Mindo, where he was researching a specific herb.

Rosa was going to jail every day with food for Segundo, who was worried about the farm. Juan had decided to stay and help out as long as they needed him, which was a relief. Rosa told Segundo not to worry, that she would start her little restaurant for the truck drivers. She had talked to Rosita, who humbly promised to help out.

With Pepe's help, they made a little lean-to near the road and bought simple but sturdy furniture at the furniture market in Quito. Rosita painted the unfinished tables and chairs in different colors and put up a sign near the road with just one word: *comida*, which is Spanish for *food*. Rosa cooked a big pot of rice and marinated a couple of newly slaughtered chickens. She was open for business! Word soon got around that her food was the best, and the need for more hands in her kitchen was a fact. Carlos, Rosita's brother, was now twelve and could easily be counted on. He would go around to nearby farms and buy green bananas (plantains), avocados, papaya, and whatever she needed. Their own production had not started yet. She had no car to drive and sell the milk the cows produced, so she decided to make cheese instead.

Four months had passed, and Rosita was getting on in her pregnancy.

John was a steady customer for all his meals. Rosita thought he was very nice. Not only did he call her señorita, which she wasn't used to, but his smile was warm and generous. She didn't understand him sometimes, but with patience, she taught him some words in Spanish. He had long blond hair tucked in a ponytail and was very tall with wide shoulders. She felt safe and protected near him. She wondered many times if she would like him to kiss her, and one day it happened. John had invited her to the research station where he worked and showed her the barrack where the personnel lived. It was prefabricated and quite comfortable. He showed her his work, and when they had entered his room, he put his arm around her and slowly drew her down on his cot. Rosita thought this was even better than when Jim had kissed her and responded happily. Now she noticed this warm feeling again. John knew she was pregnant but hadn't dared ask her who the father was or anything. He figured she would tell him when the time was right and if they would have some kind of relationship.

They spent time together every day, excitedly learning about each other. One day he asked her when her baby was due, and that opened the conversation to her story. She told him that the midwife in Mindo had said that her baby was due in August. She told him about Jim and what had happened, and she had no idea where he might be now. John had become very fond of this beautiful girl that he felt very protective of. He secretly was glad that there was no father in the picture, who was not worth anything anyway! John became friends with Rosa, who kindly accepted his suggestions about modern farming. He showed her new techniques to make cheese, which she used in combination with the local tradition, using bamboo molds and wrapping each cheese in palm leaves. With the income from the restaurant, the cheese and egg sales, she soon had saved enough to start building the house she always wanted. She planted several banana trees, and from the seeds of the papaya, she grew a *papayal* (a papaya plantation), not a big one, but she would increase it with time. She had the same plans with the dozen or so banana trees.

John helped her make a drawing of the house she wanted and inquired who sold cinder blocks in the area.

They all walked around the property to choose the perfect place for the house. Finally, the day arrived when the building of her new house was a reality. This was all thanks to John, who had supervised the planning, and Rosa was eternally grateful for his help. She was secretly hoping that his relationship with Rosita would end up in marriage. It had been her dream that her girls would marry a gringo someday, and now her oldest seemed to be close to accomplishing that dream.

Rosita's baby announced his arrival on the tenth of August, a national holiday. John ran through the woods to the midwife's house, hoping she would be home and not gone away for the holiday. Fortunately, she was home, and they both hurried back to the cabin, just in time when the water broke. John was just as nervous as though it was his own baby, and in a sense, he felt it was his own.

While he was outside smoking one of his funny little cigarettes, the women attended to Rosita and her baby.

After a while, they called him into the cabin, and from the first moment he laid eyes on the little guy, he truly felt as it was his own son. He kissed Rosita on the forehead and told her so. They were married a few weeks later. He went to register his son in the civil registry in Quito. John Maximo Swanson Quiñones—they decided to call him John after his father, and Maximo was after John's grandfather, but everyone called the boy Max.

Soon there was a date for Segundo's appeal hearing. Given the importance of the "victim," his sentence was reduced four years only. They made a deal with Oswaldo to be paid from the cheese money and over time. He accepted the offer, knowing they had no money anyway.

The cheese business was taking off like a rocket, and soon there were buyers from Quito who placed large orders. There was an urgent need for more hands to work the farm, and little by little, they increased the workforce, mainly from the area, but many brought their relatives from other places. As the population increased, it resulted in more services, stores, bars, a small drugstore, and even a dentist would come around on Saturdays. He came in his covered truck, which also served as a clinic, and walking by the square that also served as a soccer field, you could hear screams and loud suffering noises when the good dentist extracted infected molars.

Pretty soon the sleeping hamlet had grown and prospered. There was a small church, a health center, and a new school. There were two small hotels and several new eateries and a bakery.

According to the new agriculture reform deed to land had been issued, after five years of living and working on the land a permanent deed was issued. There were very few farms that had not complied with the requirements of living and working actively on their given land. Some had given up early on or negotiated their land to the best buyers. Of course, if a permanent deed for the new owner could not be presented, it wasn't a legal sale, and several fights originated. However, the rules were clear, although some inspectors would easily extend their hand for a "gift" and look the other way.

Segundo had now earned his freedom and was back at the farm.

He was very impressed by the look of his farm, which not only had a nice farmhouse but stables and other buildings, henhouse, cheese production building made of cinder block and cement, a small banana plantation, and papaya and citrus groves. An herb and vegetable gardens were producing much for themselves but also for willing buyers on market day every Saturday. Rosa had organized everything, and Segundo had to admit to himself that he was very impressed. Of course, he didn't want to tell her that, as for fear his male status would suffer. There were many resentful discussions that led to real fights. They both endured two years of constant friction and fights, not to mention Segundo's abuse of sugarcane booze that escalated the screams and even physical abuse. He left one day, having gotten a job as a cattleman on a big farm in Esmeraldas.

Rosita was now pregnant with her second child, and both she and John had trained Rosita's sister Anita how to manage the little restaurant. This way, Rosita could take better care of her health and spend more time with Max, who now needed more attention.

Max was a very smart little guy and kept close to his father. John took him on expeditions in the vast countryside on his research trips. They had a close and loving relationship; Max had not been told yet that John was not his biological father because both John and Rosita had thought it best to wait until he was older. The three were a very happy family. Rosita was sad that her father had left her mother, but at the same time, she knew that Rosa could take care of herself. She was going to be forty in a few weeks and still looked very good, even though life in the mountains was very hard, and most women her age look at least ten years older. Not in her wildest dreams she would have imagined that her farm would grow and be so successful on the day of the meeting at the nuns' school five years earlier.

WHERE IS THE TRUCK?

THREE MONTHS WENT BY, and still the rain wouldn't stop. The condition of the road was very slippery and especially dangerous. Two cars could not pass one another, and there was a rule that the first car should stop when he saw another coming up a hill. On one side, there were precipices, estimated at times to be a kilometer deep.

Pepe never complained that he had to get up around two in the morning to leave at the latest at three. In fact, I never saw him as happy as in those days. Sometimes, people would come to the house at that hour to catch a ride to Mindo or any of the other hamlets nearby. One day, Pepe and our driver, Efrain, came home in the morning without the truck. One of our charcoal customers, Doña Berta, had come with a message the day before that there had been some mechanical problem but that they were fine and would come to Quito as soon as they could. I was told to call the match factory (one of our biggest customers for *toletes*, or tree stumps). Occasionally, when Pepe had to stay overnight in the mountains and he sent the driver and the truck alone, I had been given the honor of negotiating the sale of the *toletes*. I learned something new but have often thought about this with a twinge of bad conscience. Today I just couldn't have the heart to sell the remnants of hundreds-of-years-old tropical trees to a match factory.

BYE, BYE, TRUCK

EFRAIN LOOKED FOR A place where he could relieve himself, found a spot, eased over to the passenger seat, and jumped down on the road. He took a deep breath of relief when he saw that he had parked on the very shoulder of the road and only missed the precipice by an inch or two. He started to perspire and swallowed hard. When he was finished, he turned around just in time to see the truck slowly roll down the hill and over the shoulder and down to the abyss. He couldn't move and stood there as if hypnotized.Soon he heard voices shouting from all directions. Doña Julia, who owned a bar, happened to come by in her small Datsun pickup and stopped when she saw Efrain stagger around on the road. At first, she thought he was drunk but soon realized there was something wrong with him; he was white as a sheet, and his voice sounded strange, almost whispering when he told her what had happened and that it was God's wish for him to be alive. When they got to the bar, there were many men there already commenting on the truck that had gone over the shoulder and disappeared down the abyss. The driver most likely had died on impact; they talked about the horrible state of the road and that the local government had the obligation to maintain the roads in working conditions. When Efrain came in to the bar with Doña Julia, everyone circled around him and wanted to know what happened. It wasn't long before Pepe found out what happened.

He was relieved that Efrain was alive but not so happy that he had lost the investment of the truck; in those days, not many people had insurance, so we had a total loss.

SAQUISILI

WITH OUR TRUCK GONE, Pepe decided to return to New York to work and save for about six months, or until he had saved up for a certain sum of money we needed to invest in something else. He had friends who worked at the Hilton Hotel in the banquet department and made very good money. Being alone, he was offered to share a small apartment with a friend. I told him not to worry about me and the children. We were well taken care of by my in-laws.

When I came to Ecuador, I had a burning desire for learning the language and the culture as soon as possible. I found out that there was an Indian market in Saquisili, a couple of hours from Quito. There was a bus leaving every Thursday at 3:00 am at Avenida 24 de Mayo, near where I lived. It would return in the afternoon around 3:00 pm.

There were four plazas in Saquisili (animal, produce, grains and spices, handicraft and food). Market day in the Andes is an important meeting place for people from all over nearby villages and hamlets. It is not only for trading and buying but for social interaction with friends and family members from other places. I picked Saquisili for this reason as people would talk all the time and I could listen. I could also admire the different handicrafts and learn the names of vegetables and, for me, strange fruits. I loved Saquisili from the start and went there as often as I could. It was now part of my activities, and I would schedule everything else around Thursdays. I was never afraid of not being able to get back home, knowing there always had to be a bus going back to Avenida 24 de Mayo bus stop.

My father-in-law, who had taken on the guardianship of his daughter-in-law when Pepe was gone, took his position very seriously and was not happy when I had to leave the house around 2:00 am to go to 24 de Mayo to take my three o'clock bus to Saquisili. So he would not be worried, I invited him to see me off at the bus stop. I invited him for breakfast at a small café near the stop that I had visited a few times before. Doña Clara received us as royalties and told us we should go upstairs where it was nicer. We had a generous breakfast of a bowl-sized cup coffee with milk, oven-fresh bread, fresh cheese and jam, and freshly made naranjilla juice. The taste of naranjilla is a mixture of orange, strawberry, and green such as kiwi. Hard to explain, but it is very good. The fruit is native of the Andes, not suitable for export (it ripens too quickly), but you can now find the frozen pulp (*lulu*) in some supermarkets. My father-in-law was content and left me only when the bus left the sidewalk.

Later, I heard he had told my mother-in-law, Evangelina, that since I was a foreigner, I probably could take care of myself. People would also excuse the fact that I traveled alone—something not looked well upon had I been Ecuadorian. I got as close as I could to the Ecuadorian women who did their weekly shopping. When they were finished, I would repeat the same things and was thrilled beyond belief when the salesperson would put a plateful of tomatoes in my basket and accept the money I had handed her. I always remember my first purchase, "cinco sucres de tomates." Of course, in an Indian accent, "cinco socres de tomates." I soon acquired an Indian accent too. The women of the market of Saquisili were Indians, and they were my teachers. I was saying *pes* for *pues*, *dispues* for *despues*, and so on. When I used these words in Quito, practicing my Spanish, chatting happily like a parrot, many people smiled but said nothing. Pretty soon, I had an extensive vocabulary but with an Indian accent. Some of my foreign friends went to the Catholic University to learn Spanish, and yes, they knew a lot of grammar but often called and asked me for this or that word in Spanish. When Pepe came back from NY, I still had my Indian accent, and he let out a hearty belly laugh the first time he heard me.

I knew that reading good Spanish literature would help me polish my language, so I started to read novels of Gabriel García Márquez and verses by Lorca and Neruda. Soon I was able to communicate with people on a different level, but I still think of my first Spanish teachers in Saquisili and my colloquial expressions. I still use them sometimes in a joking manner.

ILUMAN

'M NOT RELIGIOUS, AND I really haven't researched, to my satisfaction, whether witchcraft is a reality; however, I can appreciate that it is an important ingredient in many cultures. I also admit that I am curious about it. A bit north of Otavalo (a well-known marketplace in Ecuador and the home of internationally well-known Otavalo Indians) is the village Iluman, famous for its "miracle workers." Sometimes they were called witch doctors or shamans, but we used to say *brujos*. You could see one of these and be cured of whatever ailed you. Today you can see large billboards near the highway announcing how to get to shaman so-and-so. The most important shamans in Ecuador usually come from Iluman, Santo Domingo, or from the Amazon region. Many of them even have a Web page. This is a very old practice and, always, a quite profitable business. A shaman from the Amazon told me he had to keep a shaman ID card with him always. This was issued by the health ministry. not having it on him if asked by the authorities brought heavy fines.

One day, Evangelina, my very Catholic mother-in-law, asked me if I could do her a favor. Actually, it was for a friend of hers, Gloria, who wanted to go to Iluman and see a powerful brujo. Could I take her in my car? I said, "Why not? We could make an outing of it with picnic." I called a cousin, Teresa, and asked if she wanted to come too. We packed a nice basket of cold chicken, fruits, bread, and *agua de guitig* (natural carbonated spring water that is very popular). I packed other goodies too, such as figs in a spicy raw sugar syrup and fresh cheese, and off we went. It was a sunny day with an intensely blue Andean sky, perfect for a picnic in a meadow.

We arrived at José Joaquin Pineida's house. In front of his house, there were nice herb gardens and several benches arranged like in a waiting room. The shaman himself came out and greeted us, asking us to sit down on the benches. He asked if we had the gifts for him, and I produced a bag with a bottle of sugarcane distilled liquor, a couple of eggs, and a pack of Marlboro (he had asked specifically for that brand as the local black tobacco irritated his throat, he said). Then he asked us who the "patient was," and Gloria, with an anxious look, said it was she, but she wanted all of us to go in with her. The room was dark and rather musty, damp-smelling, mixed with an aroma of incense or some herb, which is common in old adobe structures without windows. Gloria sat down opposite to José Joaquin, who studied her for a few moments; he stood up, lighted a Marlboro, and took a mouthful of the liquor and squirted it out over the little table where Gloria sat. He sucked deeply on the cigarette and blew out the spray of another mouthful of liquor and a cloud of smoke above Gloria's head and the table. You could see drops of the liquor on her head and face. I noticed there were a few black stones in different shapes, of stars and other symbols, on the little table, now also glimmering of the alcohol. They really looked very old and worn, and I was told they were from before the Inca's time. After the initiating and purifying process, José Joaquin asked Gloria what the problem was.

She spoke quietly and with embarrassment, telling him that she was a widow with an only son, a medical student and very handsome. He had been a very good son, until she hired a new cook, a black woman in her forties or so. She was from el Valle del Chota in the northwest corner of Ecuador. The legend tells that in the sixteen hundreds, a slave ship capsized in the Pacific Ocean near the borders of Ecuador and Colombia. The survivors swam ashore and settled in the valley of Chota. They built their dwellings in the same manner of their homeland's customs: round huts with straw roofs. They maintained their old African customs and gathered wild plants that reminded them of home, which they later cultivated. Being free, they organized themselves and became a self-sustaining village. They practiced their homeland's customs and traditions of dances and of a drum with a tight goatskin, where they played the *bonga*, tapping with the palms of the hands in crescendo. They still do the *bonga*, adding words of recent happenings or telling stories, similar to the Spanish *coplas* or the American Rap. They also practice several African customs like white and black magic. Gloria's son had fallen in love, heads over heels, with the cook and had lately insinuated that he planned to marry her. Gloria had become hysterical and tried to talk some sense in her son, who did not change his mind. She was convinced the cook had cast some black magic on her son. Gloria tried to convince him that there were two things wrong with this relationship, her color and her age. Her son, of course, did not agree and felt that their genuine love would conquer any difficulty they could encounter. The relationship between mother and son was practically severed, which led Gloria to look for the miracle treatment from the brujo. José Joaquin looked closer at Gloria's face and said he would be back in a moment to perform the cure. She sighed with relief but shrank in her seat when, upon his return with a bunch of herbs, he told her to take off her blouse or lower it to her waist. In other words, *el brujo* wanted to see her half naked! She turned toward us with an expression of fear, doubt, and questions and pleadingly looked for a sign from us, who huddled together on a small bench.

Evangelina gave her an encouraging smile, and Gloria lowered her blouse and undergarments to the waist. José Joaquin rubbed her chest, throat, and face with an egg and took a mouthful of booze and chewed enthusiastically on the herbs. He then took a step back and sprayed Gloria's whole chest and throat with the content, which he repeated three times. I looked in awe at her expression of pure faith, oblivious of the chewed herbs that stuck to her whole upper body. With Gloria dripping wet, he then blew out a large cloud of smoke on her from his Marlboro and indicated that the cure was completed. We asked the brujo if she should dry herself first, but he shook his head and said it would work better if she didn't. He also recommended that she should put a pinch of salt and a pinch of sugar in a bottle of the *agua de guitig*, which would serve as a detox.

Money changed hands, and we said good-bye. We all walked out in the sunny but cool Andean weather and helped to dress Gloria.

Gloria was very quiet and lost in thought, with a solemn face, much like when people get their communion in church. We found a beautiful meadow close to Otavalo, where we had our picnic. Three hours later, we arrived in Quito. We dropped off Gloria at her house with many thanks and good wishes. We had hardly walked in our house before the phone rang. It was Gloria, who just had to tell us the most unbelievable thing. Since it was dinnertime, she realized that there was no smell of food cooking when she walked into her house. She went to the cook's room and found it empty. There were no clothes or personal items there. When her son came home, Gloria asked him if he had seen the cook. He said he had no idea and couldn't care less! He apologized to his mother and said he finally understood that the relationship was a big mistake, but he felt okay, no sadness, but a relief when it all came to him, like a message from above that the cook was not his real love. I called Teresa and told her; she was as surprised as the rest of us. Could we give the credit to *el brujo*, or was it a coincidence? Who knows? Anyway, we had spent an interesting day and, so as to not forget, jotted down the address to Mr. Pineida's house in Iluman. Just in case!

FLOWER CONTRACT

WITH OUR ONLY MEANS of income and the truck gone, Pepe went to New York to work for a few months. Most of my friends knew about our precarious financial situation and were on the lookout for a job or other ways to show their support. One day my friend Gladys called me and invited me for a drink in the bar in the hotel Colon. We small-talked for a while, and then she said a friend of hers would be joining us soon. Edmundo, her friend, had an eastern European accent and had lived in Ecuador for many years. He had several businesses like many European immigrants. One of those businesses was a flower shop. Edmundo was married but separated from his wife, who returned to Europe. He had a daughter who studied medicine in Texas. He went right to the point.

"I don't have much time to be in my flower shop, and I have just been asked to do a large contract for the ministry of the government. Would you be interested in doing this? I will pay you the value of the whole contract. I don't want any money myself, but they are good clients, and I want to be able to help them out with this."

"Oh yes, right up my alley," I thought. I accepted, and we made a date in the flower shop where he wanted me to work. He'd let me use whatever material I needed, the workspace, and everything. After a few days, I went to the flower shop to get the details. The minister's wife was in charge of the decorations and gifts for the upcoming Latin American convention in Quito. She had seen in a convention in Colombia that they had given the wives a beautiful basket of fruits of Colombia. The idea was nice, but she said they had to eat most of the fruits there because they would be overripe to take back home. I suggested a dry arrangement of native material from Ecuador. She thought it was a great idea and asked me what I had in mind.

I had seen many interesting branches, leaves, grass, and even flowers that looked like wood in a state of perpetual conservation. The eucalyptus tree has a flower that looks like a wooden sculpture. There is a bright orange fruit of a plant the natives called *teta de vaca* (cow tits), because that's what they looked like, the size of a lemon. I had found a couple of them in a meadow while trekking up the volcano Pichincha. I had asked a woman there if she knew where there were more of these. She told me that there were lots of them in Santo Domingo de los Colorados. They would be a beautiful contrast in an arrangement, with mostly brownish colors. There was a problem though. These fruits would rot very quickly. I decided to make an experiment and injected the fruit with *formol* (formaldehyde). I had bought it in the corner pharmacy, both the liquid and the syringe. No questions asked. I had heard that this is one of the ingredients for embalming. I know a girl who put it on her nails in order to make them harder. I don't know how healthy that can be, but she swore by it. Being highly toxic, I carefully injected a fruit. It lasted for several days in a perpetual orange state, but after a week, I noticed brown spots on it. I decided to prepare all the *teta de vaca* and used them in the arrangement. I included a small card, suggesting the receiver of the flowers to discard them as soon as they started to go bad.

I asked my friend Evelyn to go with me to Santo Domingo de los Colorados. She was an adventurous woman. She was a stay-at-home mom and appreciated a day outside the house. We went real early to be able to gather the flowers and shrubs before it got dark. We also wanted to avoid the thick fog going up the mountain in the late afternoon. I had envisioned lots of these fruits, mine for the picking, but had no idea of exactly where they would be. A Colorado Indian passed us by and said good morning, and I started a conversation with him. The Colorados (the red ones) as we called them, belong to a very old tribe called Tsachila. Their origin is the uncertain, but an anthropopogist we know, said their language is similar to the Mayans. The men shave their head, but leave some hair on top, which they cut in the shape of a helmet. They color their hair red using the seeds of the annatto fruit. Some said the reason is to keep mosquitoes away; some say it was because they like the red color and their hairstyle this way. This area where they live is quite famous for its *brujos*, especially from the Calasacon family, where most of the family members have inherited the spiritual gift. He spoke Spanish quite well, as most young *Colorados* do, and I told him I was looking for *tetas de vaca* and did he know where I could pick some. He made a sweeping sign with his hand. I looked at him with a big question on my face since there was a river in a ravine that divided the area. He pointed at a tree trunk thrown over the river and said we had to cross over on the tree trunk! He said he'd help, but he had to go to work.

I looked at Evelyn, who said, "I'm not going over there." I started to get the feel of the tree trunk, and I shouted to her that it wasn't scary at all, but she didn't believe me and stayed put while I eased myself over to the other side step by step. When I came to the middle of the trunk, with the soaring river under me, I heard a loud laugh. It was a group of young *Colorados* having a ball, pointing and watching this gringa trying to cross the river. How I made it, I don't know, but I found my *tetas de vaca*, which I put in a plastic bag. I was getting close to the tree trunk when I looked down to the river and saw the huge rocks and boulders below. There was no way out, and I had to cross over the tree trunk again. I remember my gym teacher way back then who said the best way to keep your balance when you walk on a bar was to lift your head, look straight ahead, and find a point in the horizon. With my eyes fixed on a branch, I chose a point and fixed my eyes on it, and yes, it worked. Soon I was on the other side with great relief.

Mission accomplished.

EBON AND I

Two Vikings on the Equator

A DARK BLUE MERCEDES PULLED up on the street and stopped by our house. The driver got out of the car, dressed in a dark uniform and cap. The children in the neighborhood flocked around his car and offered to take him where *la gringuita* lived, assuming he was there to talk to me. The driver was from the Swedish Embassy in Quito. He handed me an envelope with an invitation to the inauguration of the first Swedish Embassy in Ecuador. A party was just what I needed! I was hoping that Pepe would make it back in time, but he had no specific return date. Now, what would I wear? I had never been to a reception at an embassy before, but I had a black formal dress, very modern at the time, which would be appropriate, a pair of soft linden green stiletto shoes, hardly worn, and also what everyone was wearing in those days, the classic pearl necklace. I decided to spend money on a hairdresser, which wasn't much. I had long hair in those days, and I went with the popular French twist. It was simple but stylish and no fuzz.

My father-in-law was a bit anxious for my going out at night, but I assured him it would be okay. I think he had gotten used to my independent ways by now. However, he announced that he had hired a taxi with a safe, well-known driver that would be at my disposition that night. He was so thoughtful. When I arrived, I noticed that several women looked like me—blonde, with a French twist, black dress, and pearl necklace! I was probably the only one with the linden green stilettos, come to think of it. The cultural attaché and his wife looked somewhat different though. His wife, an artist, was a stunning woman with long bright red hair with straight bangs. She too wore a black dress and lots of Indian-looking silver jewelry. Later I found out that their previous post had been in Pakistan. They liked the same jazz music as we did, Thelonius Monk, Charlie Parker, Dinah Washington, etc. We became quite good friends. This is where I met Ebon. Our lives were similar, yet so different. We became such good friends that our friendship lasted a lifetime. We still talk on Skype every week. Ebon looked pretty much like me—blonde, French twist, black dress, pearl necklace. She had come to Ecuador with her Ecuadorian fiancé. Alfredo had studied in New York, where Ebon lived and worked as a nanny. We both had been in NY at the same time (I was a nanny too), but we never knew each other then.

She wasn't all that sure she would like to leave NY for good and stay in Ecuador, but her destiny decided for her, and she eventually married Alfredo, an engineer who in those days worked in the jungles building bridges. Ebon was a bookkeeper with strict Lutheran work ethics and had worked all her life. She decided to look for a job, also to make the time go faster until her man arrived once or twice a month for a long weekend. With limited knowledge of Spanish but a decisive personality, she got a job near El Ejido Park and a coffee shop owned by Frederica, a generous big German woman. It was a hangout at the time for expats. We made that our hangout too.

Ebon lived at a compound for religious employees of HCJB, an international radio station (The Voice of the Andes) initiated by an old Swedish woman, Ellen Campana, who had been there many years and was sort of an icon in the small Swedish community. Everyone called her tant Ellen. As Ebon had an evangelical upbringing, in Sweden, the compound was not really the best place to live as an adult with a fiancée, and she found a tiny apartment near her job. With limited budget, she decided to buy some furniture at the big furniture market on Avenida 24 de Mayo. That was close to my home, so we made a date to buy the furniture on market day. These were very simple but functional furniture and, of course, dirt cheap. I might add that in those days mostly single or divorced women worked, but they certainly did not live alone. Ecuador was marked as a "man's world" in many ways, and the hypocrisy was a way of life and firmly embedded in the culture. But here we were, two Swedish women fresh out of New York living in a place where a woman had to watch her ways and words so as not be marked as a wild woman of ill repute. I don't think we thought much about that, and when the group of young Indian men who helped us carry the furniture home to Ebon's little apartment were finished, we gave one of them a few sucres and asked him to run to the *tienda* (the neighborhood store) and buy some beers. I can just imagine what a nice story that made for them when they told their friends that they had drunk beer with two *gringas*!

We had trampled on a tradition by omitting several rules: (1) white women drinking beer with a group of *longos* (young Indian men), (2) women alone drinking beer with men, (3) women being alone in an apartment with men. It was just not done in those days. Things have changed now somewhat, although there still are moral guardians looking over a woman's shoulder. We are so different, Ebon and I, but maybe that was the key ingredient to our lifelong friendship. We both were thankful to have the opportunity to, in some way, preserve our Swedishness—our language, our customs, our food, and our traditions. Ebon is a no-nonsense kind of woman with both feet firmly on the ground. She would always plan ahead for sure and secure ways of getting things. One day, when we had coffee at Frederica's, she told me that the American Embassy was hiring someone with her qualifications. She was fluent in English and now had acquired a pretty decent Spanish, plus with her degrees in bookkeeping and accounting, she set out to conquer her new job interview. With her steady, confident personality and qualification, she got the job and kept it for forty years. I, on the other hand, was the one soaring in the skies, absolutely certain that the sun would always rise tomorrow!

I have always been a kind of a nature freak, preferring natural healing to orthodox medicine business. My optimism had been part of me, even before I knew what it meant. As an artist, I was told by a well-known writer who spoke some kind words at one of my art exhibition openings: "Her Nordic bleak colors have given way to an explosion of tropical colors." I think I see my life in wonderful colors, or maybe I want it to be like that. I remember once Ebon asked me if I wasn't envious of so-and-so for having more money, a better life, or whatever. But I can honestly say, I have never been envious of anybody—jealous, yes, when I have noticed somebody looking twice at my man, but that's another story!

I usually accept things as they come, uncomplicated and plain, without regrets, and I believe whatever challenge that comes, it has a good reason. In other words, what you see is what you get! Yes, some would probably call that naïve, but my courage should never be underestimated. I'm a real Viking.

Ebon loves traditional medicine. If something ails her, she looks for the very best specialists, and with total faith, she succumbs to their treatments. That unwavering faith in doctors and their medicines made her endure four years of cancer treatments, being cancer-free now. In my case, I can't say that is always bad, because once she made me go to a specialist when I was on my way to a homeopathic doctor for the second time. This time, I was glad I took her advice. I had noticed a small almond-shaped bump near my elbow. Ebon caught me feeling the bump and asked me what I had there. I explained to her that I had seen a homeopathic doctor because of it; the doctor had given me some remedies and advised me to return to him should the bump come back. After a few weeks, it disappeared, and I forgot about it. Now I had felt the bump return. Knowing me, I would probably procrastinate, so she gave me the number of a great oncologist and insisted I'd call him, who, after a biopsy, told me I had some kind of cancer, but they still needed to run some more tests.

It turned out to be non-Hodgkin's lymphoma. I remember when my daughter went with me to the doctor to inform us; he said that I most likely would not have more than up to two years of life. It was in stage 4, and he didn't give me much hope. This was in the eighties, and treatments were different then, many in the initiating-treatment stage, sort of "if it works, fine; if not, we'll try something else." The doctor said I could choose to go to Sweden, where the medicine was more advanced. He also said, "We don't have an entity here that controls the drugs for chemotherapy, which means that sometimes, we might not have them or can't get them. However, we could try to get a pilot to bring them or solicit the need by short-wave radio." Or I could go to the national cancer institute, named SOLCA, where he was a chairman of the board. If I stayed, he would be glad to supervise my treatments, which would have to be chemotherapy combined with radiation therapy. He said, "If I were you, I'd go to Sweden."

I was in shock. I had never even known a person with cancer, and I had a hard time accepting this was about me. I was faced with the decision of leaving my comfort zone, my life, my home, my family, my friends, and my art that had slowly started to take shape. It was a time of uncertainty. Did I really have to give up my life and go to Sweden for who knows how long or maybe forever? What were the alternatives really? One day, I decided to go, but the next day, I was vacillating. This went on for a month until I had a phone call from my embassy. The secretary had stated my case to the office of the surgeon general in Sweden, who urged me to take the next plane home. If I needed money, the embassy would arrange for that, but the important thing was that I would go as soon as possible. Still not decided, I went to the SOLCA with the personal note from my oncologist and chairman of the institute. I was asked to sit down and wait for a doctor to call me for an examination. I waited for a long time, and finally, I was called. The doctor didn't give me much confidence as he had a three-day scrawny beard and looked and smelled of a gruesome hangover. He asked me to go and undress in a small dressing room with a curtain covering half of the "closet" because he was going to give me a gynecological exam! I told him I was there with lymphoma diagnosis, which he ignored! I heard a little bell go off in my head, put the rest of my clothes on, and left the room as fast as I could. I sat in my car and cried for a few moments. It was quite cathartic, and I dried my tears and made the decision of going to Sweden to hopefully save my life.

When I sat on the KLM, leaving Quito, I had an empty feeling of not returning. I had a premonition of my never coming back to live in my beloved second home country.

SECOND PART

Cancer Treatments

I ARRIVED IN SWEDEN, ON a Sunday evening, and the following day, I started the hospital routines, that included a battery of horrible tests, 144 chemotherapies and 40 radiation treatments. In hindsight, it's a miracle that I didn't die from the treatments; I understand that today these are more streamlined and better tolerated now.

Being of a restless sort, I thought of what to do about my time when I was not in the hospital. This was a time when a flow of political refugees from Chile arrived. One day I went with a Chilean refugee and a friend to the information office for refugees to help her translate. We were received by very friendly personnel, and I was told there was an interpreter for my friend. Ana was distrustful and politely declined, saying that she'd prefer that I should interpret. The chief of the bureau was called and gave his authorization. When the appointment was over, he waited outside and called me into his office. His name was Toivo, an immigrant himself, from Finland, long time ago. He asked me to tell him about myself, and I told him

56

why I had returned to Sweden. After a few moments of small talk, he asked me if I would be interested to work as an interpreter on their team. I could hardly contain my excitement and said yes. I couldn't believe my luck.

I was investigated by SÄPO, the equivalence of the CIA, and got the green light shortly thereafter. Several years of translation studies began, and my preparation even took me to Spain, where I completed a program at the University of Barcelona in legal translations. Of course, I felt immense satisfaction from being useful helping people get settled in their new country.

I truly felt that my treatments and excruciating tests were a parenthesis in my life and really not the main reason for being in Sweden. Soon I was getting used to being at home again and explored my birth city, Norrköping, by bike. I rode up and down the well-known streets, taking it all in with gratitude. I reconnected with old friends and made new ones; many were from Latin America, and we still maintain our friendship by e-mail.

My job as an interpreter took me to different parts of the city, and I was on call twenty-four hours practically. I used my bike everywhere, which was more practical for my line of work. I didn't have to interrupt a delicate interpretation by having to go and put a coin in a meter! Before I started my treatments, I was fitted for a wig; a hairstylist from the salon in the hospital cut a lock from my hair and showed me a catalog, where I could choose one that I liked best.

I wore a wig during working hours, which, while riding my bike in my windy city, became a problem. Not risking it would blow away, I discretely held on with my left hand. The wig looked very natural, and very few people knew it was indeed a wig, something that surprised some clients when my hair had started to grow again and I ditched the wig, hopefully for good. My hair was now coming out real curly and evenly everywhere. My mother commented that it was even curlier than when I was a child, when I looked like a natural Shirley Temple.

I had made myself a secret promise to go to Ecuador, but without the wig. The time had come, and I told Toivo that I was going for a month. I bought a ticket in Air France, which had the best rate. Because of my treatments, I had a port-a-Cath under my skin on the chest. I was not in complete remission, and the port-a-cath had to stay there until the famous five-year window. Since it was made of titanium, I had a card explaining the hideous noise it produced at the airports. In Paris, I didn't produce the card in time, and suddenly I was surrounded by nervous guards with machine guns. Hard to tell who was most scared!

After a blown-tire incident in French Guyana and a four-hour wait, we were on our way to Quito. My family was waiting for me, and the welcome parties, Ecuadorian style, were many. I enjoyed every minute of my stay, being with my family and friends and savoring the wonderful Ecuadorian food dancing and laughing. I was feeling alive again. Everyone commented on my curly hair and gave me compliments on how well I looked. I had always had long hair, so many people were surprised to see me with short hair. The month went fast, and I knew I had to return.

This time I didn't cry in the plane when I left, because I knew I was on the road to recovery, and I would be back in my second home country again.

I had a couple more scares of the return of my malady. I got a few more doses. The side effects were detrimental and one of them affected my walking. I firmly believe in the effectiveness of natural medicine and, as my doctors had given me permission to use the medical library, I started to do serious research. I didn't know the exact doses of the herbs and the water or how much tea I should be drinking, so I brewed a large pot of two liters of water and left the tea on the kitchen counter to be sure it was all gone before I went to bed. Within a couple of weeks, I was restored and could walk normally without pain. The nurses in oncology asked for the recipe, and I gladly gave it to them!

My daughter, in Ecuador, became a widow, and as part of her therapy, she went to Spain with her little son. She stayed with friends for some time and then called me and asked if it was okay to come and stay with me in Sweden. I welcomed them with open arms. I had now stopped my treatments and was not required to go for more tests. I kept working, and she and my grandson set out to visit with my family, who they really didn't know, and they bonded right away, making up for lost time. She bought a transportation card, which allows you to travel by bus, streetcars, ferries, and train all over the province. It was nice to have someone waiting for me when I got home from work. They stayed with me for a year.

The harsh climate did not favor her well, and she told me that she had been thinking of going to live in the States. She felt much stronger now and ready to start her life again. Being an American citizen by birth, there was no problem; she and her brother had studied in the American school in Quito, so her English was perfect.

My job was freelance, so I could pretty much take off whenever I wanted. In the springtime, we went to Virginia, where she and my grandson lived with my best friend Barbara, who had a house in Crozet, a small town outside Charlottesville. The lifestyle in this country setting is very calm and slow, which was perfect for my daughter, who couldn't drive. She had to learn a lot of things from scratch since she had not lived as an adult in her country. She is very smart and soon learned how to drive, how to work nine to five, how to build a credit, and all the things we consider as normal living. Those years, I made both two and three trips to visit them. Good thing that my health was improving, and one day I was discharged if I could promise to take life easy and not work so much. I had taught Spanish and English at ABF, an adult education school, in addition to my job as an interpreter (also part of my self-prescribed therapy).

My daughter had rented a cute little house, and my grandson was now in first grade. At that time, my son was living and studying in Miami. That's when the idea of going to live in Florida entered our mind. Not only because my son lived there but because the nearness of Miami International Airport made it closer to Ecuador. Since I had no real reason for living in Sweden and since being in remission, my daughter asked me to stay in Florida. I got a very good job at a university nearby, where I worked for many years. I went on vacation to Ecuador many times. At the university, a "study abroad" program was incorporated.

One year it was a Sweden program, and I was asked to go with a group as a chaperone, together with a teacher from communications. The students should document the Swedish midsummer celebrations, very famous in the northern province, Dalarna. Since it was summer vacation, some of our students had gone home to their countries, and we all met up in Copenhagen, where we had hired a bus for the entire trip. I had asked for my vacation at the end of the trip so I could visit my family and friends. I had been fighting the flu for a couple of weeks and felt better some days, but I knew I was not completely well yet. I thought it was probably be because of the late nights, trekking in the deep forests, etc. Then it happened: I had a stroke! Since we were way up in a part of the country where there are great distances between the towns, I was rushed in an ambulance to a nearby small city. Unfortunately, they did not have the required resources for stroke treatments. I was taken by helicopter to a big teaching hospital in my province, the very same hospital I had been treated for my cancer eighteen years earlier. I stayed in the hospital for six months and one month in a rehab hospital.

I had had two massive strokes, which left me with paralysis on my left side. I learned how to walk again. This experience, as unpleasant as it was, filled me with gratitude that at least I could think, speak, read, and write. I saw many patients who could do neither.

After six months, my daughter came to take me home to Florida. I was asked by psychologists and therapists if it wouldn't be better if I stayed in Sweden. I was offered an apartment, completely handicap-equipped. I had to think about that. Most of my adult life I had lived in warm and sunny climates. In Quito, we had twelve hours of daylight. I thought of the cold and dark months in Sweden and decided to go to Florida.In the hospital I was taught to handle a stressful trip. I was walking with a crutch, but the sounds, smells, colors, people, and in general, "new" happenings could stress me out. I was unable to drive, which obligated me to stop working. I got therapies at home, and I started to paint some, but I was really occupying my thoughts with how I could get to Ecuador. The day came when I decided to go for a few months. This would give my daughter some well-earned free time. Once there and having visited with friends and family, I decided to do something. I just couldn't see my life without something worthwhile to do.

Across from where I lived was a sign of a place for rent. I inquired, and the space was perfect, and so was the rent. I had always wanted to have a Swedish café and what in Swedish we call a home bakery. This means on an artisan scale and not a big commercial bakery with sophisticated machinery. The Scandinavian colony had shrunk since I lived in Quito, but there were many people who had traveled and lived in Europe and happily became my customers. Besides, the word got out that I did not use any artificial additives and colors and everything was freshly made every day. I really worked very hard, trained personnel in customer service, and showed the bakers the Swedish way of baking our special baked goods for certain holidays. All this I did with one hand, and it really became too much for me, and sadly, I had to give it up. I certainly was not foolish enough to risk another stroke.

I went back to Florida a couple of times, and once more, I had to make a choice of where I wanted to live. A year and a half ago the infinite spirit, once again, gave me a sign of settling down. I fell and broke my femur. This placed me in a nursing home/rehab. I was told it would take some time before I could count on getting better, but probably not in the same way I was before the fall. I still spend my time painting, writing, reading, therapy, and best of all, skyping with friends in Ecuador. It wasn't in the cards that I should live my whole life in Ecuador, but I'm grateful for the years of intense living experiences that beautiful country gave me.

El chota marimba and goat skin drums photo: NS

Panecillo "the little loaf of bread" photo: NS

Panecillo with the Virgen of Quito. photo: NS

Plaza Victoria toward Panecillo. photo: Diana Bastidas

The volcano Pichincha and Quito photo: Diana Bastidas

Mariscal Sucre airport Quito photo: NS

Avenida 24 de Mayo, photo: PEN-MAG

Saquisili indian market. photo:NS

Quito and the volcano Cotopaxi photo: NS

Swedish photographerphotographer-explorer Rolf Blomberg
Long time resident of Ecuador. photo: NS

New road to Ibarra photo: PEN-MAG

Ibarra photo: NS

Imbabura Indian women photo: NS

Monument to the equatorial line photo: PEN-MAG

Kristi, Pepe, Barbara, Will photo: WC

Will, Barbara, Kristi, Pepe in Atacames, photo: WC

Pirate cave in Atacames photo: PEN-MAG

Mindo photo: PEN-MAG

ABOUT THE AUTHOR

Kristi was born and raised in Sweden but immigrated to United States, where she married an Ecuadorian and moved to Ecuador, where a new exotic world made great impression on her organized Swedish personality and way of life. She saw this new experience as a wonderful way to live life. Even though there were situations and traditions very different from hers, she looked with wonder upon the nature, the customs and traditions, the people, and the Quechua-influenced colloquial Spanish spoken, especially in the Andean region. Kristi is retired and lives in South Florida.

CPSIA information can be obtained at www.ICGtesting.com
Printed in the USA
LVOW12s1237060216

474013LV00001B/143/P